6/2028

12.c

Giant Meatball

Words and pictures by

Robert Weinstock

Harcourt, Inc.

Orlando Austin New York San Diego London

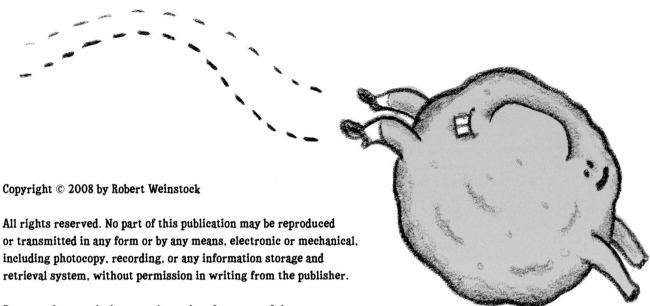

Requests for permission to make copies of any part of the
work should be submitted online at www.harcourt.com/contact
or mailed to the following address: Permissions Department,
Harcourt, Inc., 6277 Sea Harbor Drive, Orlando, Florida 32887-6777.

www.HarcourtBooks.com

Library of Congress Cataloging-in-Publication Data
Weinstock, Robert, 1967–
Giant meatball/Robert Weinstock.
p. cm.
Summary: An exuberant and overly proud meatball rolls
through town, oblivious to the destruction it causes,
until finally the townspeople decide they have had enough.
[1. Meatballs—Fiction. 2. Humorous stories.] I. Title.
PZ7.W43675Gi 2008
[E]—dc22   2007003930
ISBN 978-0-15-205595-0

First edition
H G F E D C B A

Printed in Singapore

The illustrations in this book were drawn with black
Prismacolor pencil and colored in Adobe Illustrator.
The display type was created by Robert Weinstock.
The text type was set in Pumpkin.
Color separations by Colourscan Co. Pte. Ltd., Singapore
Printed and bound by Tien Wah Press, Singapore
Production supervision by Christine Witnik
Designed by April Ward

for Dana

On the outskirts of
a snoozy little town,
not so very long ago,
there lived a giant meatball.

For years and years,

the giant meatball

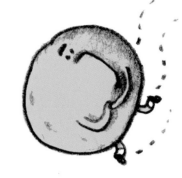

bompled and bounced his way

along the old riverbeds

When the farmer next saw the
meatball, he sheepishly asked,
"Maybe you could wait until after
my beauties are done grazing?"

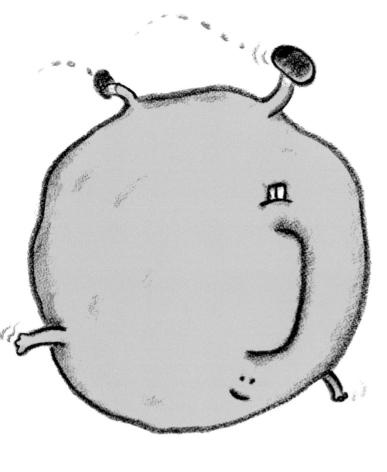

But the giant meatball was too woozy
with whirling and whistling to listen.

When the marmalade maker next saw the meatball crashing about the raspberries, he sweetly asked, "Maybe you could try not to crush so many?"

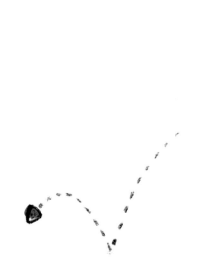

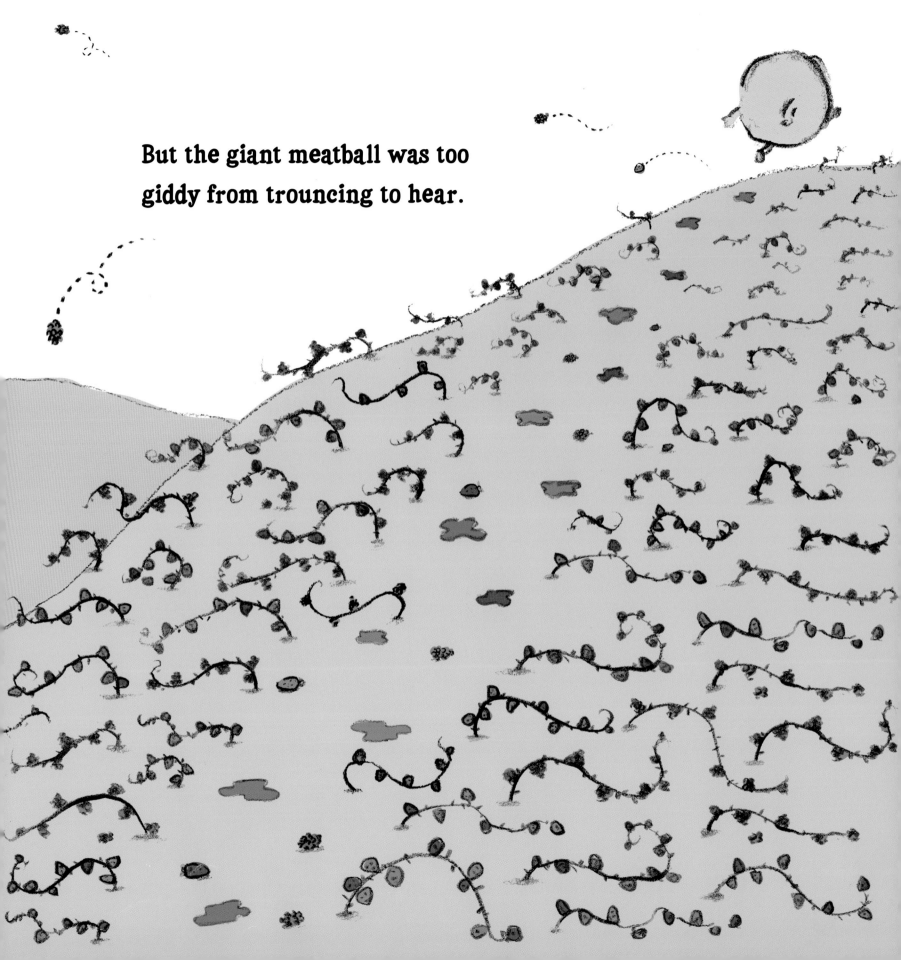

But the giant meatball was too
giddy from trouncing to hear.

And when the librarian next
saw the meatball yipping near
the public library, she put a stern
finger to her lips and shushed.

But the giant meatball was too dizzy
with the sound of his own music to care.

Ever hopeful, the mayor commissioned
the sign painter to make giant signs
with tips on neighborly living.

But the only thing the meatball
managed to read was his name.

"They love me,"

he sighed.

Flattered as he was, the giant meatball decided to whisk through the center of town.

He swerved and sloshed his way about,

sending puddles and hats

and poodles and cats flying

in his wake.

"They can't get enough of me,"
the giant meatball giggled.

The townspeople were beyond fed up.

"Let's give that meddlesome
   meatball the boot!" cried the cobbler.

"Baloney!" barked the mayor.
"I will personally give the giant
   meatball a good talking-to."

The next morning, the mayor
waited outside of town so she and
the giant meatball could talk privately.

She was still waving her arms
to slow him down when he gaily
flattened her like a pancake.

"Good gravy,"

the giant meatball bubbled.
"I must be the most scrumptious
thing ever if the mayor is
greeting me!"

And indeed he was.